the trouble with cauliflower

by jane sutton

illustrated by jim harris

Dial Books for Young Readers

To Becky, my sunshine—J.S.

To Lily Malcom, for her extraordinary patience and encouragement—J.H.

DIAL BOOKS FOR YOUNG READERS
A division of Penguin Young Readers Group • Published by The Penguin Group • Penguin Group (USA) Inc., 375 Hudson Street, New York, NY 10014, U.S.A. • Penguin Group (Canada), 90 Eglinton Avenue East, Suite 700, Toronto, Ontario, Canada M4P 2Y3 (a division of Pearson Penguin Canada Inc.) • Penguin Books Ltd, 80 Strand, London WC2R 0RL, England • Penguin Ireland, 25 St. Stephen's Green, Dublin 2, Ireland (a division of Penguin Books Ltd) • Penguin Books India Pvt Ltd, 11 Community Centre, Panchsheel Park, New Delhi - 110 017, India • Penguin Group (NZ), Cnr Airborne and Rosedale Roads, Albany, Auckland, New Zealand (a division of Pearson New Zealand Ltd) • Penguin Books (South Africa) (Pty) Ltd, 24 Sturdee Avenue, Rosebank, Johannesburg 2196, South Africa • Penguin Books Ltd, Registered Offices: 80 Strand, London WC2R 0RL, England

Designed by Lily Malcom • Text set in Horley Old Style • Manufactured in China on acid-free paper
10 9 8 7 6 5 4 3 2 1

Library of Congress Cataloging-in-Publication Data
Sutton, Jane.
The trouble with cauliflower / by Jane Sutton ; illustrated by Jim Harris.
p. cm.
Summary: Sadie must convince her friend Mortimer that eating cauliflower will not bring him bad luck.
ISBN 0-8037-2707-0
[1. Superstition—Fiction. 2. Cauliflower—Fiction.] I. Harris, Jim, date.
II. Title.
PZ7.S96824 Tr 2006
[E]—dc21   2001017333

The full-color artwork was prepared using watercolor and pencil on Strathmore rag bristol.

One night Mortimer's friend Sadie invited him for supper.

Sadie worked all day, cooking a stew.

"That smells wonderful!" said Mortimer. "What's in it?"

"I put in lots of banana skins . . ." said Sadie.

"Mmm," said Mortimer, tucking his napkin under his chin.

"And plenty of coconut meat . . ."

"Yum yum," said Mortimer, bringing his fork to his lips.

"And some cauliflower."
"Ack!" screamed Mortimer, dropping his fork.

"What's wrong?" asked Sadie.
"I almost ate *cauliflower*!" said Mortimer.
"You don't like cauliflower?"

"I like the way it tastes," said Mortimer. "It's just that whenever I eat cauliflower, I have bad luck the next day."

"Bad luck?" said Sadie. "That's nonsense."

"It is not nonsense!" said Mortimer.

Sadie asked Mortimer to just taste the stew. After all, she had spent the whole day cooking it.

Mortimer didn't want to be rude. And he *was* hungry. He tried one bite.

The stew was quite delicious! The
next thing he knew, he had polished
off four helpings.

When Mortimer got up the next morning, he stubbed his toe on the bedpost.

"Ouch! Ouch!" shouted Mortimer, jumping up and down on the foot that wasn't stubbed. "Cauliflower *is* bad luck! I never should have eaten that stew."

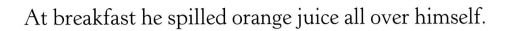

At breakfast he spilled orange juice all over himself.

When Mortimer was getting washed, he dropped his bar of soap in the toilet.

Then Mortimer remembered that it was the day of his driving test. If he passed, he would get his driver's license. He could buy a bright purple sports car with green tires.

Mortimer was very nervous about the test. He wished he had not eaten that cauliflower.

The test was a disaster. First Mortimer drove too fast. Then he drove
too slowly. He went backward when he was supposed to go forward.

Finally, Mortimer came to a sign that said: "Park Here at End of Test." But he forgot to step on the brake.

Mortimer did not pass the test. He would not be buying a bright purple sports car with green tires.

"I will never ever eat cauliflower again!" Mortimer moaned, although no one was listening.

The next day Mortimer saw Sadie in the grocery store. He told her that her cauliflower stew had brought him nothing but trouble, just as he had expected.

"Nonsense," said Sadie.

"Not nonsense!" said Mortimer. But to show Sadie he wasn't angry with her, he invited her over for dinner.

Mortimer served Sadie peanut butter and onion sandwiches.
It was the only thing he knew how to make. Sadie knew this,
so she brought along a casserole.

As usual Mortimer was very hungry. He ate two sandwiches
and three platefuls of Sadie's casserole.

"That was yummy," he said. "What do you call it?"

Sadie smiled. "Vegetable surprise casserole," she said.

Mortimer stretched happily in
bed the next morning.

I have a feeling this is going to be
a great day, he thought.

And so it was.

Mortimer went to the Summer Fun
Fair. He went on the Ferris wheel, the
merry-go-round, and the Big Thump
Bumper Cars.

He rode the Wild Alligator
roller coaster three times.

When Mortimer got home, he looked in his mailbox and found a postcard from Pete's Pizza Parlor. It said: "You have won a free pizza!"

Mortimer went straight to Sadie's house to invite her for pizza. "I had the best day!" he said. "I rode all the rides at the Summer Fun Fair. And I won a free pizza!"

"Good," said Sadie. "Now you'll get over your nonsense about cauliflower."

"Please!" said Mortimer. "Don't remind me of that horrible vegetable."

"Mortimer, what do you suppose the surprise was in my vegetable surprise casserole?"

"Not *cauliflower*!" said Mortimer.

"Cauliflower," said Sadie.

"Why didn't you warn me?" asked Mortimer. "You know that cauliflower brings me bad luck."

"Mortimer! Cauliflower has nothing to do with luck."

"Yes it does," said Mortimer. "The day after I ate your stew everything went wrong. I even failed my driving test, and normally I'm a very good driver!"

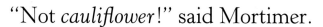

"But did you have bad luck today?" asked Sadie.

"Well . . . no . . ." said Mortimer.

"That's because you didn't expect to have bad luck."

Mortimer never liked to admit that he might be wrong.

"I'm hungry," he said, changing the subject.

Pete told Mortimer that he could choose any kind of pizza he wanted. Mortimer and Sadie ordered one with pineapple, peaches, and extra grapes.

"Oh, and put some cauliflower on it, please," Mortimer added. He smiled at Sadie.

They agreed that it was the most delicious pizza they had ever tasted.

"That pizza made me thirsty," said Sadie. "Let's get some lemonade!"
"Oh, no, I can't," said Mortimer. "Every time I drink lemonade, it starts to rain."